For Chris, P.H.

To little madams everywhere, D.A.

First published in Great Britain in 2003 by Brimax,™
an imprint of Octopus Publishing Group Ltd
2-4 Heron Quays, London E14 4JP

Illustrations © Octopus Publishing Group Ltd 2003

Text copyright © Peter Harris 2003

A CIP catalogue record for this book is available
from the British Library.

ISBN 1 85854 607 9 (hardback)
ISBN 1 85854 697 4 (paperback)

Printed in China

Perfect Prudence

Illustrated by
Deborah
Allwright

Written by
Peter Harris

BRIMAX

Prudence wasn't just best
at sums and things.

She was tops at singing...

and dancing...

and acting as well.

So when the school decided to put on "Jack and the Beanstalk", the teachers all agreed she'd make a **wonderful** Jack...

and a **magnificent** Jack's Mother...

and a **sensational** both ends of the Cow...

and even a **tremendous** Giant.

And just guess who they thought would be terrific at doing the lighting, raising the curtain, and making the CRASH sound when the Giant fell off the beanstalk?

All this didn't leave much room for
the other children in the play.
Just Karen Brown playing her banjo.

But as Prudence could play it better than her anyway, this soon changed to Prudence playing Karen Brown's banjo.

Didn't the other kids get fed up with Prudence being allowed to have all the fun? Well, they were used to it. The teachers were always saying that if a thing was worth doing, Prudence was the only one worth doing it.

As for Prudence, she never disagreed with her teachers.

The school hall was packed on the big night.
Everybody had come to see the famous Prudence.
A producer had even flown in specially from Hollywood.
The teachers were nervous. Would Prudence pull it off?

But Prudence wasn't scared. She knew she'd be a hit. She was already signing autographs and wondering what it would be like in Hollywood.

Then Prudence dimmed the lights, tuned up Karen Brown's banjo, walked onto the stage and gave the performance of her life.

As Jack, she would have brought tears to your eyes when she sold the cow.

As the Cow, she would have had you tapping your feet when it danced a jig.

As Jack's Mother, she would have had you
singing along to her duet with Jack.
(Prudence was also a talented ventriloquist.)

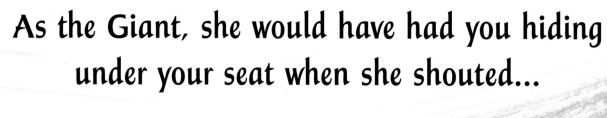

As the Giant, she would have had you hiding
under your seat when she shouted...

Yes, you would have done all those things. If only Prudence hadn't been so busy playing all the parts...

doing the lighting... and making the **CRASH** sound when the Giant fell...

... that she'd forgotten
to raise the curtain
in the first place!